The Apology

The Apology

JANET AND MICHAEL WEAVER

CFI
Springville, Utah

The views expressed within this work are the sole responsibility of the authors and do not necessarily reflect the position of Cedar Fort, Inc., or any other entity.

This is a work of fiction. The characters, names, incidents, places, and dialogue are products of the author's imagination, and are not to be construed as real.

ISBN 13: 978-1-59955-293-4

Published by CFI, an imprint of Cedar Fort, Inc., 2373 W. 700 S., Springville, UT 84663
Distributed by Cedar Fort, Inc. www.cedarfort.com

LIBRARY OF CONGRESS CATALOGING-IN-PUBLICATION DATA

Weaver, Janet, 1941-
    The apology / Janet and Michael Weaver.
       p. cm.
    ISBN 978-1-59955-293-4 (acid-free paper)
    1. Mothers--Fiction. 2. Adult children--Fiction. 3. Christmas stories.
    4. Mormons--Fiction. I. Weaver, Michael, 1972- II. Title.

    PS3623.E3836A87 2009
    813'.6--dc22

2009009604

Cover design by Jen Boss
Cover design © 2009 by Lyle Mortimer
Edited and typeset by Melissa J. Caldwell

Printed in the United States of America

10 9 8 7 6 5 4 3 2 1

Printed on acid-free paper

Dedicated to our families
Both immediate and extended.

And especially to our husband and father, Kimball, who
always believed in us.

*M*artha sat pensively looking at the memories that had been compiled in the green and red totes. In her search for the autumn home accents, she had stumbled across these items that had become her own personal inquisition. Items that, to the random eye, would only cause thoughts of Christmases past, but to her, at this time, were like a prosecuting attorney searching for answers. Her own perceptions now skewed the inquiry: "What had happened with all that time, and what was now causing time to be wasted and not relished?"

She absently ran her fingers through her gray hair with its auburn low lights and then in frustration shook her head. She paused, and turning away from the accusations contained in the memorabilia boxes, she glanced at the brown recliner to question Jim as she had done so many times in years past. But the chair sat empty, a simile of her heart.

Glancing up at the old grandfather clock, she noted the time. The evening shadows had darkened the room just as the memories had cast shadows in her heart. And so she sought solace in what had usually worked. Her favorite pro team was playing tonight, and for the next two hours, she could have a recess from the barrage of questions.

Raleigh, North Carolina, met this typical autumn day with little to make it unique. The sun rose with a crisp coolness that would slowly warm to the beauty of an Indian summer. Susan Day was preparing breakfast while encouraging her teenagers to hurry downstairs before their father hustled through the kitchen and out the door. Lyric and Michael cooperated, wanting to enjoy the few moments of his time that were allotted just for them.

"Bill, the kids will be here shortly, and we can have our morning prayer."

Not quite meeting her eyes, Bill mumbled, "Susan, I still have my prep to do before my eight o'clock class." He touched her shoulder briefly and slid out the door.

Michael lumbered down the stairs shouting, "Dad!" but only got an empty look from his mother as a response. The simple word again slipped through his lips, "Dad?"

His mother responded with a vacant look.

Lyric, not hearing her dad respond to Michael's call, knew that he had once again escaped without spending time with his family. She dragged her feet, and all of her actions demonstrated more discontent. She had experienced a great relationship with her father in younger years. He had coached her teams, and he had always been there for her church activities—the perfect dad. He had taught her about priorities, but now she wondered if his priorities were lost. Everything that he had taught her about properly placed priorities now seemed to be tied up in one of his single-tied Windsors or filed somewhere in the back of his ten filing cabinets.

Susan called, "Lyric, please come down."

Bill's new attitude was affecting everybody. Lyric's whole persona had changed from a smile and a laugh to stress lines and a grunt. Her personality once was the definition of her name. Her attitude, words, and deeds were truly the home's song. The music, now gone, left a void.

Bill drove silently through the early morning traffic. His sporadic thoughts never focused on one thing. He once had direction, but now he admitted that he was like man walking through a maze without checkpoints to let him know if he was getting closer. He could admit that he was flighty but was unable to pin down what exactly would give him stability.

He said, "Hi" and *she* said, "Hi." *She*, a pronoun that signified one thing to him and signified something else to her and to many other people in the department, the department coquet. He admitted that he flirted with her, but didn't every guy who came by do the same thing? He knew nothing would come of it, or did he? His thoughts were not as concrete as they once had been. He had once been of the opinion that a man's relationship should be nothing but business-based with female coworkers. Now some days were everything but business with her—the *she* in his life. He hid nothing—to his fault or to his credit. He walked slowly into his office to find a message already waiting. It was Susan.

"Honey, I just wanted to remind you that you have that meeting at church, and then after Lyric's activity, we need to talk about Thanksgiving and make some decisions. I love—"

"Hey, Bill, some of us are going to lunch at the Mayan. Do you want to join us?"

David, the assistant professor in the next office, paused in Bill's doorway. Receiving no reply to his question, David shook his head and moved on.

Bill began to go through his mail. He found a letter from his mother, began to read it, and then set it down. Staring into nothingness, he realized that he seldom finished anything lately—not even a phone message or a letter.

"I hope Bill's family will come for Christmas this year. I do so miss having the house full."

Martha placed a ceramic jack-o'-lantern that Bill had made in junior high on the mantle. What talent he lacked he had compensated for in his enthusiasm for the holidays. She thought of the pure joy he expressed as the first of each month rolled over and he was able to open storage boxes of appropriate decorations. That excitement was something that could only be generated from a pure love of life and true direction—a knowledge of his place in life, in a family, and in the community. He had this knowledge even as a young boy. It seemed Bill always had a self-confidence that was expressed in his desire to help others and try new things. He had truly been a delight to have in the family. She missed seeing that vision like a plough misses the spring soil.

She tried to remember some recent good times with her son, but nothing came to mind. A mother remembers everything good her child does, but it was getting so that she had to go back ten years or so to have any memory of Bill. What had happened? Was that relationship gone too?

She emailed the grandkids often, sharing her fond memories of their father. Their responses seemed to be distant recollections as well. They did reply at times and gave her some hope that they would be able to maintain a relationship. Phone calls often ended up as messages in voice mail, and Martha wondered if anyone ever bothered to push the button to get her message since replies were seldom and inconsistent.

Susan was still making efforts to stay close to the ideals and standards with which both she and Bill had been raised, but she felt as if she were fighting an uphill battle. For the last several months, Bill had shown no interest in her, their church responsibilities, or their life as a couple, and very little interest in what the children were doing.

Susan attempted to hold true to the model of family life that she and her husband had both enjoyed as they grew up in their small Montana town. Her parents had passed away in a car accident three years ago. As an only child she felt as though she was pretty much alone. Bill's family was far away, and even though she kept in touch with Bill's sister Charlotte and occasionally wrote and talked to his mother, she really had no one with whom she could discuss her concerns about her marriage. She had alluded to it in a recent conversation with Charlotte but had not wanted to share details. Charlotte had enough to worry about with her own family, and pride would not let Susan share too much of her present unhappiness.

Susan and Bill were magnets, inseparable since fifth grade. That is a long time to know who you wanted to be with forever. She was now beginning to dread the use of that word—*forever*—in connection with their relationship, because everything seemed to be one-sided. It seemed that she was the only one working on the relationship.

A week later things were getting worse. The laws of physics state that nothing truly stays the same. Everything either goes backward or forward; there is no such thing as stasis or maintaining the status quo. Bill was going backward like a marble on a hill. His latest roll backward entailed finding himself at a small cafe with *her*. He could say that he thought others would be there, but that would only be a shallow excuse.

Sighing, Martha pushed the totes to one side and made her way to the window to stare out at the swirling leaves. The nearly bare branches stretched their fingers upward and then bent inward as if trying to recapture and keep the colorful autumn foliage that had adorned them in recent weeks. It had been nearly a week since she had rummaged through the totes, but she hadn't put them away. They drew her and repelled her at the same time. Was she like those bare trees, trying to capture and keep the past at her fingertips? Slowly, she lowered herself to the floor for easier access to the totes.

She realized now that having to get up and go to work had actually been a blessing. She had retired two years ago so she could spend more time with her husband and family, but only six months later, Jim, healthy and happy most of his life, had unexpectedly suffered a massive heart attack and was gone in a matter of weeks. For a year and a half now, she had been alone.

It was true, she did have her family—her three children. Although Bill had brought his entire family all the way from North Carolina for the funeral, she hadn't seen him since and had heard from him only on obligatory days like her birthday or Christmas and an occasional guilt-forced phone call in between.

Nellie, her oldest daughter and second child, had lived in California for twenty years now, and during that time had only returned once—for her father's funeral. Why? The question had haunted her over the years. Communication with Nellie had been almost non-existent.

The only child to remain nearby was Charlotte. Her youngest child—the apple of her daddy's eye—had married Robert Pettit, a rancher, and lived about twenty miles outside of Miles City. A frown creased Martha's brow as she thought about Charlotte, her beautiful baby girl. Martha knew that Charlotte was very busy teaching school, helping her husband with the ranch, and keeping up with three active children, but she seldom dropped in, even though she had to come into Miles City five days a week when school was in session. Even a phone call would be nice. The loneliness Martha felt was almost unbearable. It surrounded her like a cloak of darkness. Was this what all parents faced when they reached her age, or was it because of her personal shortcomings and failures that she was so alone?

Upon the death of Jim, Martha had sold the ranch and everything on it. The money had allowed her to buy this home in Miles City. She had bought a bigger house than she really needed, but she had hoped that the children might bring their families and come and stay occasionally. It hadn't happened, and a lot of days she felt as lonely as if she were still out on the ranch. It was true that she had neighbors and members of the Church with whom she associated frequently, but it wasn't the same.

Bill and Susan had married while attending college in Billings, and just before graduation, Michael, Martha's first beautiful grandchild, had been born.

Martha smiled as she remembered that sweet baby boy. She had taken her vacation time and spent a week in Billings taking care of the new baby and his mom. That may have been one of the happiest weeks of her life. She and Susan got along very well, and the love they shared for that sweet baby strengthened the bond. The baby had looked so very much like his daddy had. Even now Martha breathed erratically with the memory.

Picking up a small, homemade ornament from one of the totes, Martha dangled it from her fingertips and stared at Bill's baby picture carefully glued to the round ball. What had happened between then and now? How had she failed?

Memories of her young son clamored to escape her subconscious. It was time! Martha knew she must face her past life and examine the good and the bad. Crawling awkwardly to the sofa, she pulled herself to a standing position and made her way to the basement where a box containing pictures, newspaper articles, amateur drawings and paintings, and other cherished items had been stored away for nearly twenty years.

After two days of sifting through the boxes, Martha had organized its contents into three piles—one for each child. The house was a mess; she had devoted herself to the boxes and the memories they held. She had laughed uproariously and cried silently as she had gone through each of them. Yes, the important things of her life were there before her on the floor—in three piles. She ached with the need to see her children. The pain she felt was greater than childbirth had been, stronger than when she'd had surgery on her hip, and worse than when she had buried her loving companion of nearly fifty years. There were no words to describe the wound to her heart. The tears fell unchecked as she sat on the floor cuddling "Perry," the stuffed toy parrot that had been the choice companion of all three children.

The sun had long since settled below the horizon; the street light on the corner and the neighbor's porch light had combined to cast shadows on her wall when Martha finally pulled herself up. Shoulders slumped in misery were pulled back and up as Martha walked slowly into the kitchen—determination in every step.

Somehow she must see her children. Glancing at the calendar, she realized that Thanksgiving was only two weeks away.

"Mom, look, here's a letter from Montana." Stacey's somewhat confused greeting to her mother made Nellie's heart drop and nearly stop. Her first thought was, "Now what?" She stared at the letter Stacey had thrust into her hand. It took a moment for her to realize that the handwriting was her mother's. Had it really been that long since she had seen the beautiful penmanship unique to her mother? Quickly stuffing the letter into her purse, she hugged her sixteen-year-old daughter.

"I'll look at it later. Any other mail?"

Stacey eyed her mother thoughtfully as she gave her a handful of bills and junk mail.

Glancing through it briefly, Nellie put it on the desk while asking the ritualistic question, "Honey, how was school today?"

"Okay, I guess. A kid's dad visited our Adult Roles class and talked about being a policeman, what the requirements were, and about the job itself. Miss Johnson wants us to learn about different careers. I guess it's part of the curriculum. She asked me to see when you could come and talk about being a costume designer. The girls in my class think it would be really cool to meet you. They think it sounds 'way glamorous' to make clothes for the 'stars.'"

Stacey rolled her eyes, threw back her head and struck a pose.

Nellie chuckled at her daughter's antics, "What about the boys?"

"I kind of agreed with them. Police work sounds much more exciting."

Yep, that was her Stacey. She was always more interested in action than beauty—like her grandfather. Her throat constricted at the realization that her father and Stacey had never met. It was another moment of truth as she contemplated just how much she had given up through the decisions she had made.

Stacey chattered on about her day at school and her friends while Nellie fixed one of their favorite dinners—breakfast. Sausage, scrambled eggs, juice, and toast was an evening meal they often enjoyed. This was something from Montana that Nellie shared with her daughter. The smell and the taste were like her father's hugs and her mother's smile.

Running her hands through her curly auburn hair, Nellie massaged her scalp and ended up rubbing her temples extra hard to stop the throbbing headache that had started about noon and had continually gotten worse as the day progressed. Seeing the envelope from her mother had only added to the stress.

Stacey and her mother chatted companionably while cleaning up the dishes. Nellie held her breath every time her daughter looked at her with a somewhat skeptical gleam in her eye, but a question about the letter from Montana never came up. With the kitchen sparkling, Stacey picked up her backpack (how she ever managed to lug the heavy thing around, Nellie couldn't figure out).

"Mom, I'm going in the study to use the computer for a while. Are you going to need it tonight?"

"Nope, reading this new script is all that's on my agenda. How's the paper coming on French history?"

"Pretty good, actually. It's more interesting than I thought it would be."

Nellie watched her daughter leave the room. Had her mother ever loved her as much as she loved Stacey?

Grabbing the bottle of ibuprofen from the medicine cabinet, a glass of water from the kitchen, and her purse from the end table where she had tossed it, Nellie sighed and slumped in to the comfortable green overstuffed chair. It had been a rough day at work. The dress she had designed for one of the ingénues in the latest film hadn't turned out as she had planned, and the snotty young actress had complained loudly that it made her look fat. It had taken Nellie the rest of the day to redesign and re-create the dress needed for a scene to be shot the next day. The young actress still hadn't been thrilled with the dress, but the director had said, "It will do."

Nellie sighed as she pulled her knees up under her chin and stared out the window at the lights of the city. It had been a long time since she had been able to look out a window and see trees, clouds, and sky. Yes, Los Angeles was an exciting city, but it didn't offer much in the way of the natural beauty that she craved. The high-rise apartment that she and her daughter shared was comfortable—well, maybe more than comfortable—and had a good security system, but it was just a part of the concrete jungle that L.A. had become.

She should be used to actors and actresses yelling at her, but it still hurt. She gave a bitter chuckle as she considered Miss Johnson's invitation to come and talk to Stacey's class about being a "costume designer for the stars." Actually most days she felt like a glorified seamstress. Being a costume designer was hard work, but it was also fun and almost as glamorous as she had imagined it twenty years ago when she left Montana.

Montana! She might as well quit procrastinating and read her mother's letter. Too tired to get up and get a letter opener or knife, she ripped the letter open, took a deep breath, and began to read:

> *Dear Nellie,*
>
> *It has been a very long time since I have heard from you. I hope you are doing well. I know you are kept busy with your work, but I would like to invite you to come home for Thanksgiving. I am hopeful that Bill and Charlotte will be able to bring their families and come also. Please let me know if you can make it. I would be happy to drive into Billings and pick you up from the airport.*
>
> *Mother*

Nellie stared into space as her fingers folded and refolded the note from her mother. Yeah, just "mother." No "I love you" or "Mom"—just "mother." Leaning back in the old chair, she reached over, turned off the lamp, and put her feet up on the ottoman.

Tears edged out from behind closed eyelids and coursed down her cheeks. But, why should there be any sentiment? Basically, she and her mother had had no relationship for the past twenty years. There had been phone calls on special occasions, letters (usually written by her Dad), thinly veiled requests that she come home for a visit, but very little real communication.

The guilt that Nellie had tried to keep buried in her heart rose to the surface and confronted her. She had to face it.

Graduation from high school hadn't been exciting—just a relief. Nellie's friends were all talking about college, jobs, future marriages, and exciting trips. Nellie had sat silently and listened. Her plans were not to be shared.

Nellie had barely graduated. She was not academic like her big brother and younger sister. She had taken chemistry three times before finally passing it and had ended up taking a math class (flunked in tenth grade) after school in order to get the credits she needed for graduation.

Her favorite classes had been sewing and stage crew. She had liked being involved with the kids in drama, but she was too shy to participate in much other than making costumes and painting scenery. She did go on stage occasionally as a part of the crowd scenes, but her real joy and satisfaction came in seeing her classmates wearing costumes she had designed and made. And so a dream had been born.

She had tried to talk to her parents about that dream, but her mother had looked at her like she was planning to be a "hooker" (or something equally as sinful), and her dad, although a little more understanding, had suggested that two years at Miles City Community College might help her decide for sure what she wanted to be. His desire had been for all of his children to attend college.

Bill had already completed what he could get at the Community College and had taken one semester at the University of Montana at Billings before leaving to serve the Church for two years. He was planning to get not only a BS but also a master's and a PhD.

Charlotte, two years younger than Nellie, was already making plans to be an elementary school teacher.

Her reverie was interrupted by Stacey. "Night, Mom. See you in the morning."

Stumbling to her feet, Nellie felt her way to the hall and then the bathroom before turning on a light. Ready for bed, she turned off the light in the bathroom and slipped into her room in the dark. Pulling back the covers, she tumbled into her bed, wanting some much-needed sleep, when she heard a voice in her head say, "You hypocrite. You always made sure that Stacey said her prayers while she was growing up. Sometimes you go through the motions of prayer, but when was the last time you prayed rather than just saying a prayer?" The words settled into her heart like a large stone.

She lay watching the shadows flit across the ceiling, remembering why she didn't feel worthy to pray. Yes, she went through the motions of praying, but she just hadn't felt that praying did much good.

Those unshared plans were put into play the day after her graduation. Dad was out in the pastures, checking on the cows and a few calves that were born late in the season. Her mother had gone into Miles City to her second job—as a waitress in the Hole in the Wall Café. Charlotte had ridden into town with her mother to spend the day with friends.

Nellie quickly packed the old black suitcase, which had been her father's, with as much as she could possibly cram into it. Checking to make sure that the bus ticket she had purchased earlier in the week and the money she had saved (only $300) were in her wallet, she did the thing she had dreaded most.

She rummaged through the desk drawer where her mother kept bills, business receipts, and extra checkbooks. Tearing out one check from the book, she sat down, and while looking at a cancelled check from the drawer, she copied her mother's writing and signature. She now had in her possession a check for $1,000 written out to "cash." She had purchased the bus ticket earlier in the week when the person on duty was someone she didn't know, but everyone at the bank knew her. Would her plan work?

Visibly shaken, Nellie placed a previously written note on the kitchen table, gathered her things, and went out to the old beat-up Ford pickup. Yes, the keys were in it, as always. Now, if it would only start. She was hopeful that there was enough gas to get her into Miles City.

Taking a deep breath, Nellie entered the bank with what she hoped was a natural smile on her face and approached the first available cashier. "Mom asked me to stop in and get this cashed."

The teller looked a little surprised at the amount but handed her a pen, asking her to endorse the check. "Looks like you guys are going to be doing some big spending."

Nellie swallowed hard before answering: "We're going to Billings tomorrow to pick up some equipment Dad ordered. They asked that we bring cash."

The cashier accepted her explanation without question, counted out the cash, and with a smile said, "Well, be careful and have a good trip."

Fighting the urge to run, Nellie had walked slowly out of the bank to the old Ford truck and driven to the bus depot. She arrived just in time to hop on the bus. Her plan was going to work.

Nellie groaned at the memory and pummeled her pillow as she tried to find a comfortable position so she could get some sleep. And still the feeling came that she needed to pray. Finally, she rolled out of bed and knelt to petition her Heavenly Father.

"Dear Father," she whispered. "Please help me. I need forgiveness for the many wrong things I have done in my life. I need to know what I should do next. Bless my mother and bless me. Help us to build a relationship. Help me to be honest with my family. Please, please help me."

The tears streamed down her face, and even though she had made the same plea from time to time in the past, she had never quite had the same feelings of peace as she had now.

Emotionally and physically exhausted, she fell into bed to sleep undisturbed by memories or dreams.

Charlotte stopped at the mailbox at the end of the lane, and Bobby jumped out of the car and got the mail. Hustling back to the warmth of the car, he tossed the mail into the backseat before reaching down to retrieve one letter that had fallen into the snow.

"Hey, Mom, this looks like a letter from Grandma. Why would she be sending a letter instead of calling?"

"Who knows?" muttered Charlotte as she accelerated to get out of the muddy and half-frozen spot in the road.

Without another thought about the letter, Charlotte and her children gathered up the mail, bags of groceries, backpacks, and Bobby's trumpet and hurried into the house. A sudden storm had turned the Montana air frigid.

With dinner over, the dishes cleaned up, and the children in their own rooms supposedly doing homework, Charlotte kicked off her shoes, gathered up the mail and school work she had brought home to correct, and sank into the old but comfortable rocker by the fireplace. Robert had gone out to the barn to check on a sick horse and to chop more wood for the fire. Bobby and Steven had carried in the last of the chopped wood.

Charlotte smiled as she thought of her two boys (the spitting image of their handsome father). They emulated their dad's work ethic and tried so hard to help. Nancy, her oldest child, tried to help around the house, too. She had always wanted to help her mom, but Charlotte worried. Was Nancy getting enough time to be a child? Was she going to make friends and be involved in school activities next year when she went to Miles City High?

Charlotte sighed. They tried to give the children advantages the kids who lived in town had, but the very fact that they lived out on the ranch was limiting. She knew what it was like to be lonely for close neighbors and friends. That's the way she had been raised. Ranch life was difficult, but she and Robert had chosen it when he inherited his dad's ranch. Yes, it was a good life, in spite of the difficulties.

Thumbing through the mail, she quickly discarded most of it, put the bills in a pile, and then opened her mother's letter. Why in the world would she write?

> Dear Charlotte,
> It has been some time since we really talked. I hope you are doing well. I would like to have you and your family come to my place for Thanksgiving. I am hopeful that Bill will bring his family and that Nellie will come also. I hope to hear from you and/or see you soon.
> Mother

Confusion was the main emotion Charlotte felt as she carefully reread her mother's note. Had it really been so long since she had seen or talked to her mother that her communication had to come in the form of a formal invitation? Instead of beginning the never-ending job of correcting papers, Charlotte leaned back, closed her eyes, and tried to remember when she had actually conversed with or seen her mother.

"Wow!" She was startled to realize that it had been nearly six weeks since she had seen her mother and that she had only talked briefly with her on the phone once since then. Six weeks ago, her mother had followed them home from church and had dinner with them, and then Charlotte had called one snowy, cold day to see if her mother needed anything from the store. The call had been very brief since Charlotte was anxious to grab a few groceries and head for the ranch before the snow got any deeper.

Charlotte appreciated the fact that her mother respected their privacy as a family and tried very hard not to interfere or impose—the two main reasons she gave for not asking Charlotte to do anything for her. However, sometimes she just wished her mom would be a little more demanding or at least call. Then Charlotte realized that the few times her mom had called her in the recent past, Charlotte had been in a hurry to get somewhere or do something and had cut her mother off with, "I've got to go now. I'll call you soon." No wonder her mother had quit calling!

When Charlotte and Robert had gotten married, Charlotte

had just graduated from college with a degree in elementary education. Robert still had one more year of school left before he got his degree in agribusiness. Charlotte had been hired to teach in Miles City, so Robert decided to make the drive into Billings every day to finish school. Graduation was approaching, and Robert had been applying for jobs elsewhere when his father died, leaving him the ranch. It had been a joint decision for them to live on the ranch, which happened to be fairly close to the Day's ranch, and for Charlotte to continue teaching. Robert's mother moved to Glasgow to live near her only daughter.

Charlotte's memories were interrupted when Robert came into the house. Noticing that she was curled up comfortably in the chair with papers on her lap, he gave her a gentle kiss and offered to see that the kids had finished their homework and get them to bed.

With a smile and a quiet "thank you," Charlotte started to grade papers but couldn't keep her mind on the task at hand.

Yes, life had been good to them. There wasn't a lot of money, and they had struggled, but both she and Robert had been doing something they enjoyed, and they had three beautiful children. Was that the way her mother and dad had felt?

Charlotte had always been a planner, so all three of their children were born in April. That meant six-week maternity leaves and then the whole summer to love those babies. Most of the time Robert was able to take care of the children while she was at school. And her dad was always willing to pitch in when needed. The more she thought about it, the more she realized that her mother often changed her work shifts around in order to help out, too. The children had loved going to "Gwampa and Gwama's." When her mother had retired from nursing and only worked at The Hole in the Wall occasionally, the children sometimes played sick in order to miss school and go to the grandparent's home for a day.

Then "Gwampa" had passed away suddenly, the children were all in school, and her mother had moved into town. The children were healthy, and Grandma's services had seldom been needed.

Her mother was probably very lonely. *Duh, what gave you your first clue?* Charlotte asked herself as she picked up the brief note and read it again.

Reading between the lines, she tuned in to her mother's feelings as a wave of guilt washed over her. Her mother probably felt that they only wanted her when they needed her to do something for them. That wasn't true at all! How could she have let her busy life make her push her mother's needs completely into the background?

Charlotte focused in on the line "I am hopeful that Bill's family and Nellie will be able to come, too." The yearning in that one simple sentence nearly broke Charlotte's heart.

"When pigs fly!" she muttered. Bill called her once in a while to check on their mother, but it was usually Susan who showed real interest. Bill was so terribly wrapped up in his professorship, committees, and his published articles that he seemed to be thinking only of himself. Charlotte wondered if his indifference was cast upon Susan and the children also. She hoped not. Until recently she had felt that Bill had it all—a beautiful wife and children, a high status job with decent pay, and a strong relationship with the Savior. However, after talking to Susan the last few times, she wasn't so sure.

As Charlotte searched her thoughts, she realized that there had been moments when she hadn't thought it quite fair that Bill and Nellie had escaped Montana for adventure while she had remained to face the harsh winters and the responsibility of their parents. However, as she had matured, she realized that it had been her choice and that there had been far more benefits to her situation than drawbacks, and probably the biggest benefit had been the relationship her children had with their grandparents.

Again Charlotte stared at her mother's note. She and Robert were planning to take the children to Glasgow to spend Thanksgiving with his mother and sister, but if there was any chance that her siblings might come, she would beg out of the traditional trip to Glasgow. Bill might (and that was a big might) come, but there was little chance that Nellie could or would.

The clock chimed ten o'clock—much too late to call Bill and Susan on the east coast, but she might reach Nellie.

Nellie noticed the light flashing on the telephone as she and Stacey hurried out the door to school and work. Funny, she hadn't heard the phone ring. It must have been last night after they went to bed or this morning while she was in the shower. She had overslept this morning, and she'd just have to check the answering machine when she got home. She hesitated for a moment, wondering if the call might be from her sister, but Charlotte always called her on the cell. In fact, Nellie had never given Charlotte her home phone number, just as she had only given Charlotte her business address. Stacey was holding the door to the elevator open and tapping her foot impatiently. "Come on, Mom! I'm going to be late."

Letting Stacey out at the entrance to the private school where she was a sophomore, Nellie lingered to watch her daughter join a crowd of friends and enter the building. She was thankful that she made enough money to afford this school. It had been difficult and worrisome when she had enrolled Stacey in one of the inner-city schools as a first grader. But by the time Stacey was in sixth grade, Nellie was making enough money to afford the school Stacey now attended.

Pulling out of the parking lot, she headed for the costume shop, which was only a couple of miles away—another plus for the school.

The traffic was heavy as usual at this time of day, and Nellie kept her attention on the road as she swiftly covered the distance to work in her new corvette—another sign of her success.

Parking her car in her designated parking place (almost as good as a key to the executive washroom), she took her time getting to her office. The costumes for their latest film had been completed, and today she was going to have the seamstresses (her assistants) clean the shop while she read the new movie script and got some ideas for costumes for it.

Settling in a chair by the corner window, she opened up the script and began to read. An hour later, Nellie put the script down, stretched, and rubbing the back of her neck, reached for her purse. She needed a stick of gum or something to nibble on to keep her awake. Her hand settled on an envelope. She had forgotten that she had shoved her mother's note in her purse and that her mother had both her home and business address. She opened the letter and read it again as she paced around the office. "No, there's no way! I wouldn't—couldn't—take Stacey, and I'm certainly not going to abandon her on Thanksgiving."

The script was completely forgotten as Nellie sat down to contemplate just how she had reached this point in her life—success, yes, but at what price?

As the Greyhound bus had eaten up the road between Miles City and L.A., Nellie had become less frightened about being hauled off the bus by the police for forgery and more frightened at what lay ahead of her. Was she a fool? She had really wondered if her parents would send the police after her. She was eighteen, but she had also forged a check. That was against the law. There was one part of her that wanted the police to find and take her to the safety of home, but another part of her wanted to make it not only to California but to her goal—success. She breathed a sigh of relief after every stop.

Arriving in L.A. tired, ragged, and scared, she had clutched her suitcase and purse close to her, and praying for guidance (all the time wondering if she were worthy of help after what she had done), she found a place to stay for the night. A little thought in the back of her mind kept resurfacing: *Is someone else praying for me too?*

Nellie had pushed those memories back for so many years that it almost made her ill as she mulled over the memories of those early times in L.A. Somehow she knew she had been guided as she found a cheap, but clean room in a somewhat safe area of the city, and she had found a job in a small restaurant.

She had written to her parents telling them that she was safe and that she was sorry about what she had done but would send them the $1000 as soon as she could. Her return address on the letter resulted in an immediate reply written by her dad, thanking her for the letter and saying that they were glad she was safe. Not a word was said about the money, and it was signed, "We love you! Mom and Dad."

For the next year, she had worked her shift at the café and spent the rest of the time making the rounds of the costume shops showing her portfolio of sketches. Finally, her break came—she landed a seamstress job in one of the major shops, and after six months of part-time work, she was given a full-time position, was able to quit her job at the café, and move into a better apartment. She received regular letters from home, usually written by her dad, but always signed "Mom and Dad." Bill had written occasionally, and Charlotte wrote regularly.

She sent her parents a check for $200 with her first full-time paycheck and sent another $200 every paycheck until she had paid them back. Even then, nothing was said about the money. The checks were cashed, and the next letter always said, "We are glad you are doing well. We love you!"

It was at this point in her memories that Nellie wanted to close down, but the memories kept coming.

Terribly lonely, she had been swept off her feet by a young wanna-be actor who rushed her off to the Justice of the Peace for a quick wedding. She hadn't let her family know what she had done. Her sister Charlotte had gotten married about the same time, but Nellie had not been able to go. The filming of the latest movie they were costuming had been pushed ahead, and since she was a newlywed and the sole bread-winner in the family, it was impossible for her to miss work and the paycheck.

She had wanted to take Dylan home to meet her family, but he had vetoed the idea every time she mentioned it. Only six months after Dylan had moved into her apartment, she knew she had made a terrible mistake. He accomplished little as he tried to cover up his inadequacies with fruitless behavior. He was a parasite, and all parasites take from their hosts, physically and emotionally. How big of a chunk would she allow him to take from her?

Nellie realized that she would never take Dylan home to meet the family. In fact, she would never tell anyone that there had ever been such a man in her life. She was getting a divorce. She had missed Bill's wedding and now she truly felt like a failure. While her brother and sister had wed and were beginning their lives and their families, she had a train wreck that had started before "I do" and was ending with him doing nothing.

Nellie had packed Dylan's clothes, put them out in the hall, rekeyed her locks, gotten a restraining order, and contacted an attorney about a divorce. Then the big blow came. Her attorney could find no public record of any marriage taking place. She didn't need a divorce because she had never been married!

Dylan's clothes sat in the hall for several days before he came to pick them up. Ignoring the restraining order, he had tried to unlock the door. When his key didn't work, he began pounding and yelling.

Furious, Nellie had opened the door to confront him.

Dylan leered as he stumbled into the doorway, drunk as usual. "Well, Mrs. Livingston, or should I say 'Miss Day'? Are you getting a divorce?"

Nellie glared at him. "How could you do that to me? You knew I would never let you move in without being married! You have no worth because you care nothing for the value of others."

Dylan chortled, "John did a pretty good job acting the part of a Justice of the Peace, didn't he?"

"John?" He was one of Dylan's friends, one of the rummy bunch who took up residence in her apartment while she was at work. No wonder he had smirked every time he looked at her. Now she understood some of the innuendos he was constantly making.

Gritting her teeth, Nellie demanded, "Get out! Get out now before I call the police."

"Ah, baby, come on. We're in Hollywood. Everyone lives together without being married! Let me come home."

Taking advantage of his drunken state, Nellie shoved him out of the doorway, slammed the door, and called the authorities to remove him like the cyst that he was.

It was two weeks before she heard from him again. The phone rang, and not recognizing the phone number on the caller ID, Nellie answered.

"Hey, babe. They finally let me out of the slammer. Can I come home?"

The words chilled her as the Montana winds never had. She quickly hung up on him, denying him any further communication.

She knew that she had let him father her child, but also knew that she would never let him be the child's father. She would do it on her own, and on her own she was once again.

Nellie thought of the joy Stacey had brought into her life and how lonely it would have been to have lived these past sixteen years without her. She hoped she would be forgiven for her errors and often wondered how she, who had done so many things wrong in her life, could be blessed with such a wonderful daughter. Luckily, by the time Stacey was born, she made enough money to afford the nice high rise apartment in which they now lived. One of the seamstresses at the shop had become one of Nellie's best friends. She was a better babysitter than she was a seamstress, so Nellie had hired her. A lot of the time during those first few years, Nellie took Stacey to work with her, and the friend had tended her there. It had worked out very well.

From that point on, Nellie threw herself into her work, and it paid dividends. The thrill of her name on the credits of the first movie for which she had been head costume designer still made her tingle with excitement. The only event in her life that had been more exciting was when she had held that beautiful baby girl with a mass of auburn hair in her arms. That had been the highlight of her life. Stacey was her life!

No, she didn't regret having Stacey. She did regret the way it had happened. She also regretted not sharing Stacey with her family. She had told Stacey that she had grandparents and relatives in Montana but that it was too far away to go and visit. Stacey, with the simple faith of childhood, had accepted that and let it go. But Stacey was no longer a child, and Nellie found it increasingly difficult to evade questions about the past and Nellie's family.

Only Charlotte knew of Stacey's existence. About six months earlier, Nellie had been in the shower, and her cell phone had been left on the kitchen table. When the phone rang, Stacey picked it up.

"Hello?"

There was a pause before a tentative "Nellie?" was heard.

"Nope, this is Stacey. May I give her a message?"

"Yes, please ask her to call Charlotte."

"Will do! I'll have her call you, Charlotte, as soon as she gets out of the shower."

As Stacey pushed the end button, she heard a slight gasp and turned to see her mother standing in the doorway, toweling her hair dry.

"Mom, someone named Charlotte just called. Wants you to call her back. I'm going over to Jean's place for a while if it's okay."

"Sure, just be back by one. Remember, you have a dentist appointment."

Nellie stared at the door as Stacey closed it behind her.

Now what? How would she explain Stacey to Charlotte? Well, might as well get it over with. Picking up the cell from where Stacey had laid it, she called her sister's familiar number.

"Hi, Charlotte. What's up?"

" 'What's up with you?' is the better question," replied Charlotte, somewhat bewildered. "Just who is this Stacey who answered the phone?"

Silence on Nellie's end had made Charlotte probe a little more. "Well, who is she? What's the secret? Does she live with you? She sounds young, and I don't think you've ever mentioned her before."

A dozen possible explanations went through Nellie's mind— she was a friend's daughter; she was a neighbor who just dropped in; she was the director's or producer's daughter. But Nellie was so weary of covering up. She wanted—no, she needed—some family support, and so the truth, the whole truth spilled out into her sister's listening ear.

Charlotte's initial reaction had been shock, but after Nellie had explained the situation, she had simply said, "Nellie, you need to call Mom."

Nellie's feelings of guilt and embarrassment surfaced, and she asked Charlotte to keep her secret—just for a little while longer.

"Oh, Nellie, Mom loves her grandchildren very much. She will forgive you and love your daughter just as she does my children and Bill's. Our girls need to know each other."

Now, Nellie was again facing her own deceit. When her father had died, she told Stacey that Grandpa was dead. Stacey adamantly argued with her mother. She wanted to go to Montana for the funeral. With the family's grief over the death of their beloved husband, father, and grandfather, now was not the time to share her secret. Luckily, Stacey's choir teacher had insisted that everyone be there to compete in the solo ensemble festival that was being held that week. Stacey had relented and stayed with a friend and fellow member of the choir.

Nellie had been shocked at how much her mother had aged and thrilled to see her nieces and nephews, but she felt hollow as she realized that Stacey should be there too, getting to know her cousins. Using the excuse of a new movie that needed costuming, she had flown in the day of the funeral and out the day after.

And now, her mother wanted her to come home. She just couldn't do it.

Interrupted by Jean, her assistant, she left the past behind, answered Jean's question, and went back to reading the new script.

The phone was ringing when Stacey and Nellie entered the apartment that evening. Nellie quickly reached for the phone.

"Hello, sure just a minute." Turning to Stacey, she whispered, "Sorry, it's the director of the new movie I'm working on. Could you start dinner while I talk to him? The meat loaf is in the fridge.

Turn the oven to 350 and put the meat loaf and a couple of pota-toes in. Okay?"

Looking somewhat perplexed, Stacey went to the kitchen and did as she was asked. Then she glanced at the telephone extension with a question in her eyes.

The voice on the other end of the phone made Nellie smile. She loved to hear from her sister. It was sometimes the only stabi-lizing thing in her life.

"Hi, Charlotte. How come you called me on the home phone? I didn't know you even knew the number."

"There seems to be something wrong with your cell. My calls wouldn't go through, so being the resourceful little sister I am, I called information. I don't have to be a rocket scientist to figure out how to do that."

"Is everything okay in Montana?"

Then the question Nellie dreaded was asked.

"Nellie, did you get a letter from Mom?"

"Yes."

"Well, do you think you could possibly come for Thanksgiving?"

A long silence followed.

"Nellie, don't you think it's time you rejoined the family?"

"Charlotte, you know I can't. I certainly won't leave Stacey alone, and I can't face Mom with what I have done."

"Oh, come on, Nellie. You aren't sixteen any more. Give your mother some credit. She isn't stupid, and she certainly isn't as judgmental as you seem to think she is."

A long pause and then, "Is Bill coming?"

"I don't know yet. He was out of town at some kind of conven-tion. Susan said they would talk about it and let me know, but she was afraid they couldn't make it on such short notice. You know, Nellie, we've both felt that Bill and Susan have the perfect life, but now I'm not so sure."

The two sisters talked for a few more minutes before Nellie said in a tear-choked voice, "Charlotte, I just can't come. I'm not ready. I'll write mother and tell her I'm starting to costume a new movie—which I am—and just can't get away."

Charlotte hesitated and then whispered, "Oh, Nellie, please don't wait until we have another funeral to come home. Don't let Mom die without meeting Stacey, and don't deprive Stacey of a relationship with her grandmother. I love you."

The phone went dead. Nellie stared at the receiver as Charlotte's last words rang in her ears.

Stacey gasped in disbelief and shock. She had never listened in on one of her mother's phone conversations before, and now she almost wished she hadn't heard this one. Her mother had acted so strangely since she got the letter from Montana, and she had sent Stacey from the room after she answered the phone (not her usual method of operation). Curiosity had gotten the best of Stacey. Waiting until she heard her mother hang up the phone in the other room, she gently cradled the receiver back onto the hook. Quietly she dashed up the stairs to her bedroom.

Wow. She had just heard her aunt's voice. She had cousins. She had uncles! Unable to digest all this information, she flopped on her bed. Gazing at the ceiling, she went through what she had heard again: "rejoin the family—mother not judgmental—Charlotte, I just can't come." What in the world had her mother done that was so terrible?

When she had been old enough to realize that she didn't have a dad like other kids, her mother had told her that things had not worked out between her and her dad, and so it was just the two of them. Nellie had said that she had kept her maiden name and that's why Stacey was Stacey Day. At the time, Stacey had not thought there was anything strange about it. A lot of the kids she knew were in the same situation. Names and fathers didn't seem to be really important. Now she began to wonder.

Dinner was quiet with Nellie and Stacey each lost in her own thoughts.

What other secrets has my mother kept from me?

Later in the evening, Nellie got in the shower and Stacey quickly checked the caller ID and wrote down the number. Listening to make sure her mother was still in the shower, she rummaged through her mother's purse, hoping to find the letter that had come in the mail a few days before.

Pulling out the crumpled letter, she wrote down the return address and hesitatingly pulled the letter from the envelope. Her grandmother wanted her mother to come for Thanksgiving, but she had said nothing about Stacey. Suddenly Stacey knew the truth. Her grandmother didn't know she existed! What was her mother's problem? Tears fell fast and furiously as she stuffed the letter back in the envelope and put it in her mother's purse.

A quick shower, pajamas, and then Stacey was in bed pretending to be asleep when her mother came in to say good night. After her mother left the room, Stacey lay awake for a long time thinking about all that she had learned and all she didn't know. When she was little, she had wanted to write to Grandma and Grandpa. In fact she had written some letters, but she never got an answer. Had her mother even mailed them? Mom had always answered her queries about not receiving letters with, "Oh, they are probably just too busy." Stacey had soon quit writing and had quit thinking about those mysterious grandparents who were just "too busy."

She had wondered if her mother ever heard from them. Maybe her mother had given them her work address when Stacey got old enough to read. But why had this letter come to their apartment? Too many questions and not enough answers.

Dear Bill and Susan,
    It seems so very long since I have heard from you and much longer since I have seen you. Michael and Lyric are probably so grown up that I wouldn't recognize them. I hope

you are all well. I know that you are very busy and that your vacation time is limited, but I would like to invite you to come home for Thanksgiving. I am hopeful that Charlotte and Nellie will be able to come. It would be wonderful if we could all be together again. If you can come, I would be happy to drive to Billings and pick you up at the airport.

Mother

Bill stared at the familiar writing. If his mother knew what was going on in his life right now she probably wouldn't even want to see him.

Just then *she* poked her head in the door.

"Bill, could you give me a ride home? It seems that I just missed the last bus."

"Sure!"

As they left the building on their way to the car, a cold Carolina rain began to fall. He opened the door and she slid in before he dashed around the car and popped in behind the wheel.

Driving through the drenched, leaf-strewn street, he knew that he could forget all his concerns by simply talking with her, but where would this conversation lead?

With just a couple of blocks to go, the car swerved and the sound of rubber on the wet road changed to metal. Bill jumped out to view a completely shredded tire. He leaned against the door as she rolled down the window slightly. "It looks like we're walking."

They hustled to her front step where the porch light paled the dreary street and the torrid current in the gutter. Entering the house, she shed her soaked jacket and strolled to the hallway, removing her drenched yellow blouse as she went. "I need to get out of my wet clothes."

Returning seconds later, she threw Bill a towel and suggested that he get out of his wet clothes as well.

Bill took off his wet polo shirt and, wiping his hair and face, tried to soak up the water that clung to his T-shirt. From the other room, she asked, "Would you like something warm to drink?

Wrapping the towel around his neck, he answered, "Sounds good to me."

Wearing a white camisole and light green cotton pants, she returned with two cups of hot chocolate. She sat down next to him—in fact, the only way she could have been closer to him was if she had been the towel wrapped around his neck.

Turning toward her, he took both drinks from her hands and set them on the end table. At that moment a picture of her and a man was the focal point of his vision. Quietly, he questioned, "Who's that in the picture with you?"

"Oh, that's just my father," she said with a smile.

Her father! It could have been anyone but her father.

Like lightning, a lesson his father taught him many years ago came to his memory. It was a Friday night and Bill was heading out for the evening. "Remember son, a man makes decisions every minute that define his character. How are you going to define yours?"

He left without pause or hesitation!

Martha stared out the window at the bleak street. The clouds were gathering, symbolic of the clouds threatening to engulf her heart. It was a week before Thanksgiving, and she had hoped to be shopping for baskets and baskets of food with which to feed her family. Instead, she was wondering if there might be some lonely soul from Church who might need a place to spend Thanksgiving. She had purchased a small chicken and a few other items, but her Thanksgiving dinner would be pretty sparse.

She tried to fight back the tears, but finally just let them fall. Besides, no one was here to see them. She had received Nellie's short note explaining that a new movie was in the works and she simply couldn't get away. Bill had called, saying it was too far to come for the short time he had off from his responsibilities at the University, and Charlotte, the only one who seemed genuinely sorry, had come by with the kids Saturday and insisted on taking her to lunch before explaining that they already had plans to go to Glasgow.

Martha sat down in the brown recliner (Jim's chair), pulled the afghan around her, and quietly cried, "Oh, Jim, was I such a terrible mother? What did I do that was so wrong?"

Some time later, Martha pulled herself together as she realized what Jim would say, "Hey, what's wrong with my girl? You've always been strong. Now is not the time to quit. Things will work out."

After she had sent the Thanksgiving invitations to her children, Martha had spent all her time compiling their memorabilia into three different scrapbooks with the idea of presenting them to the children at Thanksgiving time. She had finished Bill's and was about through with Nellie's.

Her stubborn little jaw stuck out determinedly as she made up her mind to finish the project and give them to the children as Christmas presents.

Susan sat staring out the window at the chilly winter day in North Carolina. It sounded funny, but in Montana this day might be considered "downright warm." That's the way her dad or her father-in-law would have said it.

A smile lit her face as she heard Bill rumbling around upstairs. She couldn't quite put her finger on what had happened, but Bill had been different this last week—almost like the Bill she had married. It had all begun that night of the terrible rainstorm. He had come home late because of a flat tire. He had entered the house dripping wet with a strange look on his face. Traipsing across the kitchen floor, leaving rivulets of water with every step, he had come to the table where they had just begun to eat. As she turned to chastise him for his tardiness and the wet floor, he had leaned down and softly kissed her. "I love you, Susan." Then turning to the children, he had smiled. "I'm going to get into a hot shower, and then I'll be down. Go ahead and eat."

Now it was the day before Thanksgiving, and she could hear Lyric and Michael stirring. Quickly setting the table and putting some eggs in to boil, Susan began rolling out pie crust in preparation for the next day.

Lyric bounced down the stairs. Her song was back. "Dad and Michael are wrestling up in Michael's room. Honestly, Mom, don't boys ever grow up?"

Susan chuckled at her teenage daughter's growing wisdom. "Not really! Dash back up and tell them if they don't come down to breakfast now, they'll have to wait until lunch."

"Yeah, as if that would happen!" Lyric's tone of voice showed that she knew her mom was joking.

The smell of turkey wafted up the stairs and pulled Lyric and Michael out of their beds. Bill sat contentedly reading the paper while Susan basted the turkey and began mixing up the hot rolls.

"I still wish we had been able to go to Montana for Thanksgiving," said Lyric, sighing. "All of my friends are going to their grandparents' homes. If it's just us, it will be pretty much like any other day, and I know Grandma invited us. I bet she's lonely today."

"Hey, sis, you know dad said the vacation time was just too short to go that far."

"I know, but there's always some excuse. Grandma's going to forget what we look like."

Susan and Bill exchanged a smile as they heard their children's discussion on their way down the stairs.

Several hours later, Bill's family sat down for the Thanksgiving feast.

Bill looked lovingly at Susan and then turned his attention to Michael and Lyric.

"Before we offer thanks for all our blessings, I would like to say something."

Michael and Lyric grimaced at one another. Dad was infamous for his long speeches while they anxiously salivated over the delicious spread. This time they hoped he would keep it short.

Clearing his throat, Bill paused and looked intently at his family. The children were beginning to shuffle uncomfortably. "I just want you to know that I am most thankful for the three of you. I love you very much. I know that you wanted to go to Montana for Thanksgiving." He stopped and looked at Susan. "I have a surprise for all of you. How would you like to go for Christmas?"

Stunned silence met this question, and then everyone began to talk at once.

"Really?"

"Do you mean it?"

"When would we go?"

"Are you sure?"

"Oh, that would be so cool."

"That would be great. Can I call Grandma and tell her?" questioned Michael.

Bill felt a warm rush of satisfaction, "Well, I thought it might be fun to surprise her."

It was December 17 and the bitter cold air from Canada had settled into Montana, accompanied by a big snowfall. Martha stayed inside and finished the scrapbooks. Many memories surfaced as she worked, and she felt impressed to write them down. In each book was a written account of their lives as she remembered them.

Each memory included an account of that child's birth and her feelings at that time, as well as accounts of their childhood exploits, their achievements in school, athletics, extracurricular activities, their graduations, and their activities beyond high school. In each one she expressed how much she loved that child and how proud she was of him or her.

Still not satisfied with the project, she sat down at the computer and wrote the following:

Dearest children,

The only thing I ever really wanted to be in this life was a good mother. As I have put together your scrapbooks, I have reminisced over my life, and as I see what my life is at this point, I feel that for the most part I have failed to achieve what I wanted to be, and so I offer you my apology.

Bill, I'm sorry I wasn't able to attend all your sporting events, that I missed your awards banquet when you received "Most Valuable Player" on the football team. The day you graduated from high school, I came in late because I had been with a dying patient at the hospital. So many times work interfered with my attendance at important events in your life. Your Dad was there, and I guess I thought that would be enough. He always proudly shared with me every detail of missed events, but I realize now that I was the one who missed out. If I could turn back time and do it over again, I would find a way to get out of work and be there with you.

And, Nellie—my dear, sweet Nellie. I'm sorry I was not more understanding and supportive of your dreams. Being busy and preoccupied might be excuses, but they certainly are not good reasons. When you left Montana, my heart went as well. It was then I began to shut myself off from everyone. I gave up feeling. I was surviving. I am so very proud of you and your accomplishments. I have kept a list of every movie for which you designed the costumes, and I've seen saw most of those movies. I am sorry that I didn't act more appropriately when you left. I'm sorry I never made coming out to California to see you a priority. Somehow I could have rounded up the money. I'm sorry I've never told you how much I love you and how terribly much I've missed you. When you left, part of me died, and it affected how I reacted, not only to you but also to Bill and Charlotte. To all three of you, I apologize. I should have been stronger. I should have handled things differently.

Oh, Charlotte, I'm sorry that I buried my emotions in my work and didn't take as much interest in you and your *activities as I should have. I am so proud of you and your wonderful family. When your father died, it took another part of my heart. I know I have neglected the children's activities, and I could have called you occasionally instead of sulking when you didn't call me. I am so sorry. Please forgive me.*

Yes, children, I know I have failed you all in different ways. I hope you will understand that it was not intentional.

Our Father in Heaven loves us all unconditionally, and I want each of you to know that I may be a little disappointed in some of your choices, but I will never, never stop loving you.

Mom

Martha quickly printed off three copies of the letter and slid them into envelopes before she could change her mind. The doorbell rang.

"My word," she mumbled. "Who could that be?"

It was just dusk, and she could barely make out the figure standing on her porch as she looked out the window in the top of the door. "Good grief, it looks like Nancy, but Nancy never rings the doorbell, she just bounds in."

Opening the door, Martha stared at the young girl shivering on her doorstep. In a coat much too light for Montana weather and with a suitcase by her side, the girl, who did indeed look like Nancy (same age, same hair color, but a little taller), stared back at Martha with an indiscernible but pathetic look in her eyes.

Without a second thought, Martha reached for her suitcase with one hand and pulled the girl through the door with the other hand. "My word child, get in here before you freeze."

Stacey gazed at this woman who was her grandmother. How she wanted to throw her arms around her and tell her who she was. However, she didn't know about her grandmother's health, and she certainly didn't want to cause a heart attack. Then, too, maybe her grandmother wouldn't want her.

"Are you Mrs. Day?" Stacey finally questioned after a long silence.

"I am, and who are you? How did you get here?"

"I'm Stacey."

"What a pretty name, but Stacey who?"

"Da—Davis."

"Well, Stacey Davis come on over here by the fireplace and get warm, and then we'll see what I can do to help you."

Martha gently pushed the girl into the chair by the fire, took an afghan from a nearby sofa, and wrapped it around the girl's legs.

"I have some hot chocolate on the stove. Let me warm it up a bit, and I'll bring you some."

When Martha left, Stacey looked longingly around the room. Three 8x10 photos were equally spaced above the fireplace. She immediately recognized the middle one as her mother—her mother when she was probably about her age or a little older. The boy on the left must be Bill—"Uncle Bill"—and the girl on the right must be "Aunt Charlotte."

Her heart pounded so hard she was sure her grandmother would hear it in the other room. Would her grandmother believe the story she had rehearsed and was about to tell?

Stacey silently sipped the mint-flavored hot chocolate, putting off any conversation. Martha watched the girl with curiosity. *Who is this beautiful little waif, and why is she here?*

Finally, she could stand it no longer. "Okay, Stacey, what's going on? What can I do to help you?"

"You can let me stay here for a few days," she said, gulping.

"I can what?" demanded Martha.

And then Stacey told the story she had carefully rehearsed on the bus trip from Billings. She and her mother were going to Canada to see her grandparents for Christmas. They had left California on the Greyhound bus several days ago. Her mother hadn't been feeling well, and when the bus stopped in Salt Lake, she had gotten off to find some medicine, but she had told Stacey that no matter what happened she was to stay on the bus until she arrived at their destination. Her mother didn't return, and even though Stacey had tried to tell the bus driver that they needed to wait for her mother, he had said he couldn't "get off schedule."

Martha interrupted her to ask why she had gotten off in Miles City and if she knew where her mother was.

Stacey kept her eyes on her hands folded neatly in her lap as she continued. "Well, you see, I had a cell phone and my mom called me right after we left Billings. She was calling from a pay phone in Salt Lake. She said that she had fainted while looking for medicine and that she had been taken to an emergency room at a nearby hospital. They had insisted that she stay overnight for observation, but she's fine now and should be on a bus headed this way."

"Well, I'm certainly glad she's all right, but why did you get off the bus in Miles City, and how did you get to my place?" Martha interrupted.

Stacey paused and looked at this woman whom she had wanted to meet for so long. Somehow she didn't believe that she "had been too busy" to answer a child's letter. She knew now that her mother had never sent the letters. *Why?*

Taking a deep breath, Stacey went on with her story. "Mom told me to get off at Miles City, get a motel room with the credit card she had given me for emergencies, and then come back to the bus station and wait for her tomorrow, but when I began searching through my purse, I discovered that both my credit card and cell phone were gone. I must have left them on the bus.

"I started to cry. A woman came over and asked me what the trouble was. I explained my situation, and she said that there was a Mrs. Day who lived only a few blocks away from the bus station who was really nice and kind, and that she lived all alone. She said she thought maybe you would let me stay here for a few days until my mother caught up with me."

Somewhat skeptically, Martha asked, "And just what's the name of this lady who thinks I run a boarding house?"

"I—I—uh . . . don't know. She didn't tell me."

Stacey stared at her feet as Martha looked her up and down. *The girl's story could be the truth, but it was full of holes, too. Is she a runaway? Will she steal things?*

At this thought, Martha chuckled. *Not much in this house worth stealing, and how would she carry it away? Her suitcase is almost more than she can handle. And she certainly doesn't look like a murderer. Am I being foolish?*

And then Martha's thoughts reversed to twenty years ago. Her Nellie had left home, and oh, how she had prayed that someone would be kind and helpful to her. She made up her mind.

"Okay, Stacey. You can stay until your mother gets here."

Without thinking, Stacey lunged from her chair and threw her arms around Martha. "Oh, thank you, thank you!" And then the pent up tears of fear and happiness flowed like a river. There seemed to be no dam strong enough to stop them.

Martha hugged the girl close and a tear or two of her own dropped as she patted the girl's back.

It was 10 PM when Stacey snuggled into the bed. Before turning out the bedside lamp, she looked around the cozy room—a little old-fashioned perhaps, but the chintz coverlet and curtains as well as the daintily flowered wallpaper shouted the message that this room was for a girl. She had prayed, thanking her Heavenly Father for her safe trip and for finding her grandmother.

Still too excited to sleep, she pulled the lamp chain and rolled over to look out the big window. She was amazed that she could actually see the sky with the moon and stars shining brightly through the window. The twinkle was brighter than all the lights of L.A.

L.A. and her mother. Suddenly she felt very guilty, but if her plan worked, it would all work out. Her mother would rejoin her family; she, Stacey, would meet that family; and she would make her mother tell her the truth about everything. She was sixteen now. She could face facts. She didn't need to be protected.

After listening in on her mother's phone call and reading her grandmother's letter, Stacey had been really upset and had hardly spoken to her mother for several days. Then a plan began to form in her mind. She knew that if her mother had kept her a secret for sixteen years, she was not going to reveal her overnight.

School would be out on December 15 and wouldn't resume until January 4—a nice long holiday. Nellie was generous with her money, and since Stacey wasn't a spendthrift, she had a considerable amount in savings. Taking the car to run some errands for her mother, she had gone to the bank on Saturday, withdrawn most of her money, and then gone to see her friend's mother who was a travel agent. Explaining that her Mom was busy and had sent her to make some reservations, she purchased an airline ticket for herself to Billings, Montana, for December 16, and one for her mother for December 23.

December 16 was a work day for her mother. That made it easy for Stacey to enlist the aid of a friend to take her to the airport. When she left, she placed a note and the airline ticket on the table where her mother would be sure to see it.

The flight to Billings was a piece of cake. Making it to the bus station and catching a bus to Miles City was a little more difficult. She had to sit in the bus station five hours before the scheduled bus came through, but now she had reached her destination.

Stacey smiled, snuggled deeper under the covers, and went to sleep. Things would work out.

"Stacey, Stacey, are you here?" Only silence greeted Nellie's call. Too bad! She had gotten off work early with the idea of taking Stacey Christmas shopping. Stacey had probably gone shopping with a friend.

Nellie went into the kitchen to look for Stacey's note. That was the number one rule in their house. If either one of them left while the other one was out, a note had to be left on the kitchen table.

Nellie smiled as she picked up the note. The smile gradually faded as she read.

Dear Mom,

You asked me what I wanted for Christmas. I said a trip to Montana. You said no, and so I'm giving myself what I want most. I want to see Grandma, Aunt Charlotte, Uncle Bill, and all my cousins. (Nellie gasped—what?—how?) Yes, Mom, I know. I'm sorry, but I listened in on one of your calls from Aunt Charlotte, and I read Grandma's letter inviting you for Thanksgiving. I'm sorry, but I needed to know. And when you're ready, I really need to know why you haven't shared your life with me and why you haven't told your family about me. Are you ashamed of me? Don't worry. I know what I am doing. I am flying to Billings, and then I will catch the Greyhound bus on to Miles City. By the way, your Christmas present is in the envelope on the table. See you soon! I love you!

Stacey

In shock, Nellie slowly read the note again before opening up the envelope containing an airline ticket to Billings, Montana, on December 23. The flight left L.A. at 11:05 PM.

Nellie paced back and forth in the kitchen. Stacey knew. Stacey was gone! Would her daughter ever forgive her? She felt like a giant sieve was squeezing her size 10 figure into a size 4. Had her mother felt that way when she ran away from home nearly twenty years ago? How cruel, how cruel! Nellie now realized just what she had put her parents through. She certainly hadn't been fair to her parents. She had said, "Sorry," but had she really apologized?

She tried to recollect what she had said in the note she had left her parents. Something like, "I'm going to taste my desires. I'll let you know when I have an address. Why can't you understand me?" Actually, as she remembered, it was probably a very cruel note.

And with that note she had begun a life of deceit. She had made a real mess of her personal life, and in spite of her successful career, she was not proud of the reflection she cast. Stacey was the most important thing in her life, and she had really muffed that relationship by not acknowledging her and giving her the extended family she deserved. Nellie spent the next hour berating herself for all her wrongs. Finally, worn out emotionally, she dropped to her knees to pray for forgiveness.

Rising from beside the chair, she called Charlotte.

"Hello, Charlotte Pettit speaking."

Silence, and then Nellie's quivering voice. "Oh, Charlotte, what have I done? Can I ever repair the heartbreak I've caused?"

"Nellie, Nellie, is that you? What on earth has happened?"

Words tumbled out quickly as Nellie confided in her sister. When she finally paused for a breath, Charlotte broke in:

"Hey, it may not be as bad as you think it is. If Stacey is anything like you, she's resourceful, brave, intelligent, and a survivor. She'll be a lot safer on the plane than she would if she were making that long trip by bus. Sorry! I know you made the trip on a bus, but things were different then."

"Oh, Charlotte, I was such a fool. Why did I put my family through what I'm experiencing now? Do you think Mom will ever forgive me? Can you forgive me? Can my daughter forgive me? Do I have the right to ask for forgiveness?"

The silence was palpable as Charlotte soaked in Nellie's anguish. How could she comfort her sister? Looking up, she made a silent plea that she might say the right thing.

"Oh, Nellie, the family forgave you many years ago. From what you have told me, Stacey is quite mature for her age. She will be angry for a while, but yes, she will forgive you. And, Nellie, of course you can receive eternal peace and forgiveness. That is why Christ came to this earth. That's why we celebrate Christmas. He came that He might atone for all of our mistakes. The Savior suffered for you, me, and everyone else."

There was a pause as Nellie could be heard quietly sniffling. Finally, she said, "I'll call you back later."

During the next call the sisters decided that there was no way Stacey could reach Miles City before the seventeenth, but they didn't know what time she had flown out of L.A. Charlotte would start checking bus schedules.

The empty silence of the apartment reverberated in her ears and heart as Nellie lay sleepless in her bed that night. She had called Stacey's cell phone several times, but there was no answer. The battery must be dead, and Nellie had discovered Stacey's charger still plugged in on her dresser. However, her sincere prayer for her daughter's safety, as well as a petition for forgiveness, had left her with a feeling of peace.

Stacey slept late. She was physically and emotionally exhausted. As she lay in bed looking around the room, she discovered various photos of her mother and Aunt Charlotte. It seemed like they must have enjoyed each other and spent a lot of time together. It would be fun to have a sister. She could hear her grandmother humming Christmas songs as she bustled around the house. Stacey's happiness would be complete if only her mother were in the twin bed on the other side of the room. Stacey hoped her mother wouldn't let her anger veil the peace and joy to be found in Grandma's house.

Yawning and stretching, Stacey reached for her robe. She needed to face this dear lady whom she desperately wanted to call grandma, but she didn't feel like she could continue to stay here under false pretenses. What would she do?

Pulling out the phone number she had taken from the caller ID, she considered calling Charlotte. That might be the best idea. Charlotte at least knew Stacey existed.

Hearing her grandmother go outside, Stacey hesitantly dialed the number on the extension in her room.

A young girl answered the phone: "Hi, this is the Pettit residence."

"Hi, is your mother home?"

"Yes, she is. May I tell her who is calling?"

"This is Stacey."

"Mom," whispered Nancy, "there's a girl who wants to talk to you. She sounds kind of nervous, but says her name is Stacey."

Charlotte smiled as she took the phone from Nancy. "This is the call I've been waiting for. I'll explain in few minutes."

"Hi, is this Stacey?"

"Yes, are you really my Aunt Charlotte?"

"Sure am. I talked to your Mom about an hour ago, and I've been waiting for your call. Where are you? I'll be right there to get you."

"No, it's all right. I'm at Grandma's, but she doesn't know who I am, and I just can't go on lying to her."

"You're where?"

"At Grandma's."

Completely dumbfounded, Charlotte asked again, "But how? And when did you get there?"

Quickly, Stacey told her aunt the details. By the time she finished, Charlotte was chuckling, "You certainly are cut from the same mold as your mother, and I can't wait to see you. Look, your mom is really worried about you. She has called me three times since she found your note. I was supposed to call the bus depot after every arrival and see if you had gotten off. I guess you got here sooner than we thought you would. Nellie is going to call your grandmother and fill her in on your existence and everything else. I suggest you lie low until after she gets that call, and then simply give your grandmother a hug. I think she is going to be happily surprised. I'm going to tell your cousins about you, and then we are going to come right into town to see you. I can't wait."

With a relieved smile, Stacey echoed those sentiments, "Neither can I!"

It was morning, and Nellie had gotten off the phone with Charlotte only moments before when the phone rang again.

"Nellie, she's here, she's safe, and she's with Mom."

"She's where?"

"With Mom!" Charlotte laughed as she envisioned her sister's face. "I know; I asked Stacey the very same question when she called me a few minutes ago. I said, 'You're where?' Can you believe your daughter's ingenuity? She just walked into her grandmother's home, entering her grandmother's life, without causing her a heart attack."

Charlotte quickly filled her in on what Stacey had told her, ending with, "Nellie, call Mom now!"

"Hello, Martha Day speaking."

"Mother, it's me, Nellie."

"Oh, Nellie, it is wonderful to hear your voice. Is everything okay? You sound uh, well, a little uncertain."

"Yeah, I—I'm fine, but Mom, I need to tell you something, something I should have told you sixteen years ago. I, I hope you'll forgive me."

"Oh, Nellie, I forgave you a long time ago. I'm sorry you've been worrying about that all these years."

"I never really felt like you had forgiven me, but now I have a secret that I need to share, and for which I'll need your forgiveness again."

"Nellie, please just tell me. You've got me worrying now."

Gulping for a breath of air, Nellie began: "I understand you have a young teenager there who showed up on your doorstep last night."

"How on earth could you know that?" interrupted Martha.

"I just know. But, Mom, why did you take her in?"

"Well, it was cold. She had no place to go. And to tell you the truth, she reminded me a lot of you twenty years ago. I remembered how hard I prayed that someone would help you. And I figured maybe I was being given a second chance—a chance to help a young woman since I hadn't been able to help you!"

"Mom, just listen, please!" Nellie interrupted. "That girl is Stacey Day, my daughter."

Martha gasped and then listened as Nellie poured out the

whole story. When she finished, she paused, waiting for her mother to say something.

After a long, long silence, her mother spoke through her tears. "I knew she looked like you. She's beautiful and sweet, and I love her already."

There was another pause while both women wiped their eyes and struggled to regain their composure.

"Nellie, when will you be here?"

"Christmas Eve. I'll rent a car in Billings. And, Mom, I, uh, I love you. Thank you."

Leaving her bedroom door ajar, Stacey listened anxiously for the ring of the telephone while she made the bed and straightened up the room. When she heard the telephone, she hopped into the shower. She couldn't stand to listen to her grandmother's side of the conversation. What if she were angry and didn't want anything to do with Stacey? Stacey couldn't stand the thought of that. To find her grandmother and then lose her would be unbearable.

When she finally felt brave enough to venture out, Stacey turned off the shower, toweled herself dry, and slipped on her robe. Slowly opening the door to the bathroom, she looked out to see her grandmother standing with hands on her hips.

"Well, well, young lady. You certainly pulled a fast one on your old grandmother," and with her stern face lighting up in a smile, she pulled Stacey into her arms. Stacey felt an intense joy to think that her grandmother had accepted her immediately, and this acceptance made it all feel real instead of surreal. "Let's get you unpacked. You're here to stay for a while."

For the next week, Stacey basked in the love and attention that only a grandmother can give. They decorated the house, put up a Christmas tree, and baked cookies galore while sharing stories and love.

Charlotte's family came into town several times and spent hours—hours that were precious to Stacey as she became acquainted with her cousins. She and Nancy were able to become friends because they had not known each other as cousins; their relationship was unique just like the situation. Nancy stayed over several nights, sleeping in the other twin bed in Stacey's room. They giggled and talked for hours, relishing their new relationship. They cherished every moment they had together.

Stacey and her mother had talked on the phone two or three times. All of the conversations were pretty much about the family and everything that was going on in Miles City, but the big question, why? lingered unspoken between them, causing a gulf that they had never experienced. Nellie knew she and her daughter would have to talk.

"Was Grandpa a real cowboy?" questioned Stacey as she and her grandmother finished cleaning up the kitchen after having spent the morning making and decorating sugar cookies.

Martha smiled. "Oh yes. He could break broncos with the best of them, and he was always happiest when he was astride his bay mare, Brownie. They were a team, those two. Brownie was a cutting horse, and all you had to do was hang on and let her take her head when trying to cut a cow out of the herd."

"I've always loved horses. Now I know why. I wish I could have gone riding with Grandpa."

"He would have liked that. Your Aunt Charlotte often rode with him. Your mom rode when she was little, but lost interest when she reached high school. Bill rode a lot, but it was mostly because he had to in order to help on the ranch. I'm not sure he ever really enjoyed it."

"Grandma, do you have some pictures of Grandpa on a horse?"

Quickly, Martha wiped her hands on a paper towel. "I think we're finished in here. Come into the living room."

Reaching up on the shelf that contained several scrapbooks, Martha pulled down the worn brown one, and opening it, turned the pages until she came to one that contained only one big picture labeled "Jim and Brownie."

Stacey and her grandmother stared at the picture in silence.

Both shed silent tears as Stacey thought of what might have been and Martha remembered what had been.

Finally, Stacey broke the silence. "Wow! Grandpa was a man's man! No wonder you fell in love with him."

Martha chuckled. "He was twenty-five years old in that picture, but he wasn't too bad looking in later life either."

"Brownie is pretty, too, and look at that saddle. It looks like it could have been used in a movie."

Suddenly, Martha remembered something. Putting the scrapbook down on the sofa, she grabbed Stacey's hand and pulled her toward the door to the garage.

Turning on the light, she pointed Stacey toward the north east corner of the garage.

Stacey gasped. "Grandpa's saddle!" A few quick steps and she was caressing the smooth leather of the old saddle that sat on a saw horse.

"I couldn't bear to part with it. Maybe someday I'll give it to one of the grandsons, but for now I like it here where I can see it." Martha stepped up beside Stacey, and while putting an arm around her added, "Or maybe a granddaughter!"

It was then that Stacey noticed a wide leather strap with bags attached to each end. It was lying on the saw horse behind the saddle. "What's this?"

Martha picked it up. "This is a saddle bag. I didn't know it was here. Robert moved everything from the barn. He took a lot of the stuff to his place to use, but when I requested that the saddle be brought to my garage, he must have brought the bag with it."

"A saddle bag? What is it used for?"

"Carrying lunch, an extra change of clothes, or anything else one might need or want to keep close."

As Stacey worked at opening one of the bags, she remarked, "They aren't very big. They don't look like they would hold much. Hey, wait, there's something in here!"

She pulled out a notebook and about six envelopes. As she handed them to her grandmother, they were both surprised to find that three of the envelopes were sealed, and labeled, "Nellie," "Charlotte," and "William."

Recognizing the precious handwriting, Martha grasped the envelopes as if she were reaching for Jim one more time.

Stacey watched Martha for a few minutes before quietly asking, "But, Grandmother, why would these letters be in the saddlebag?"

Shaking her head, Martha answered, "I'm not sure, and I don't know why I didn't think to look in there." Then turning toward Stacey, she continued, "Your grandfather was a master of the written word. I think he actually found it easier to communicate that way. He always carried a notebook and pen in his saddlebags. When he was riding the range, he often took time during lunch or even at night around the campfire to write down his thoughts and ideas. He even dabbled in poetry, and he penned more than one sweet missive to me while he was away."

Stacey opened up the notebook. "You're right. Look at this cowboy poetry. It sounds pretty good to me. Grandpa must have had quite a sense of humor, too."

Martha smiled, "That he did!"

"But, why didn't he send these letters to my mom and aunt and uncle?"

Thoughtfully, Martha stared at the envelopes. "Now I remember. Your grandfather had just spent three days rounding up cattle. When he came home, he complained of not feeling well. He came right into the house, showered, ate a little supper and then went to bed. It was when he awakened in the night that he had the heart attack from which he never recovered. He must have written those letters during that trip and just forgot about them. However, I do remember now that just before he died, he said something like, 'Sorry . . . the children . . . letters.' I was upset and had no idea what he was talking about. He must have been trying to tell me then."

Stacey wrapped her arms around her grandmother and pulled her close. The two women were united by a man whom the younger had never met and the older would always love.

Moments later, after having searched the other bag and discovering candy wrappers and a pen, they took their treasures back into the house.

Martha observed Stacey seriously reading the poetry in the notebook as she alternately smiled and surreptitiously wiped away a tear or two. "Stacey, would you like to have that notebook?"

"Oh, yes. Could I? But what about my cousins? Won't they want it?"

"They have their memories. You should have this."

"Thank you, thank you so much!" Then Stacey added with a smile, "Won't Mom, Aunt Charlotte, and Uncle Bill be surprised and happy to get these unexpected Christmas presents?"

"Stacey, what a great idea! I'll just tuck these letters in with the presents I have for them and put them under the tree."

Stacey watched as her grandmother looked again at the letters in her hand. "Grandma, is something wrong?"

Martha smiled pensively. "No, I was just thinking about your grandfather and how he always encouraged me to share my feelings and thoughts, yet he was the one who left his feelings in the saddlebag.

It was early on the morning of December 24. The big sky was clear and was pronouncing its legendary status. Nellie shivered with delight. She was home. No smog marred her vision of the airport sitting up on the flat ridge above Rim Rock in the middle of Billings. As the pilot coasted onto the landing strip, Nellie unbuckled her seat belt before the seat belt light turned off, and grabbing her carry-on luggage, she was down the aisle and at the door before the plane came to a full stop. The stewardess started toward her, but seeing the excitement on Nellie's face, didn't have the heart to stop her.

Nellie jogged down the runway into the building and headed for the luggage claim area. She hadn't brought many clothes, but she had brought lots of presents. After claiming her baggage, she looked around for car rentals and hurried in that direction. She hadn't reserved a car but was sure that there would be one available. When she reached the desk, she was told, "Sorry, we only have one car left and that has been reserved. If you want to wait around, we should be having some come back in a few hours."

What choice did she have? Picking up a sandwich from Burger King, she made her way back to take up residency in a chair near the rental booth. The girl working there said she would make sure that she got the next available car. Then the clerk had asked a very poignant question, "Are you visiting or coming home?"

Nellie had answered without hesitation, "Coming home."

"I have a reservation for a small SUV. Is it ready?"

Turning with a start, Nellie stared in the direction of the voice. "Bill," she shouted as she dashed forward and flung herself at the man at the counter.

Automatically throwing his arms around her, Bill Day stared into the eyes of his little sister.

After the reunion, Bill herded his family to the SUV. Nellie was surprised at how Michael and Lyric had matured, and their smiles were like never-ending hugs. Eventually they had all their luggage stacked onto the top of the car and were on their way to Miles City. Susan, Lyric, and Michael had generously insisted that Nellie take the front seat by her brother and had kept up a steady stream of excited chatter.

"Bill, does Mom know you're coming?" Nellie asked.

"Nope, it's a surprise!"

Nellie took a deep breath. "It seems to be the season for surprises, and I have one for you."

It became silent in the car as everyone looked at her expectantly.

"I have a sixteen-year-old daughter. Her name is Stacey. You'll meet her today."

Without going into much detail, she simply explained the situation and that she was terribly sorry that she had never told them about Stacey.

Bill pulled off the road and stopped the car, apparently still unable to do more than one thing at a time. "Why did you do that to yourself? Why did you carry that burden on your own? Nellie, I'm sorry that you didn't feel you could come to me." Reaching over the passenger seat, he hugged his sister reassuringly. Nellie clung to him, savoring the feel of love, family, and protection.

Once they were back on the road, Nellie looked at Bill and realized that he was still a good-looking man. She smiled as a fleeting memory surfaced. She was a freshman in high school and Bill had taken her to his Senior Cotillion. It was her first formal dance, her first date. Bill had taken some razzing from his buddies, but his concern had been for his little sister, and he had made her feel like a princess.

Coming back to the present, Nellie heard the excited voice of her niece. "Yes! I have another girl cousin about my age. Stacey, Nancy, and Lyric! This Christmas Holiday is looking better by the minute."

Laughter and questions followed as they traveled the rest of the way to Miles City.

It was 3:00 PM, and Nellie still hadn't arrived. Stacey and her grandmother were both afraid she might have changed her mind about coming. As they exchanged looks of concern, Martha looked out the window to see a car drive up. "Stacey, I think your mom's here. That's strange. There seems to be others with her. Do you have any idea who it would be?"

"No idea at all, Grandma," Stacey answered as she lingered in the doorway, not quite sure how to greet her mother or how her mother was going to greet her. Martha was too thrilled to worry. Dashing outside in the cold without even grabbing the old gray jacket she kept close at hand, she slid to a stop as the doors opened and Bill, Susan, Michael, Lyric, and Nellie all tumbled out of the car. All the family was home.

"Stacey, get out here and meet your other cousins."

Explanations ensued as they dragged the luggage out of the cold and into the warm house.

While waiting for the arrival of Aunt Charlotte's family, Lyric, Michael, and Stacey tentatively explored their new relationships. Excitedly, Lyric and Stacey discovered that they had many things in common, including their tastes in music, the desire and ability to sing in their school choirs, and, of course, liking boys.

When Uncle Robert drove up with his family, Michael and Lyric hid behind the front door while Stacey went out to help her cousins carry in their contribution to the traditional Christmas Eve dinner. The dinner almost ended up on the floor when Michael and Lyric jumped out yelling "surprise!" The family finally sat down to enjoy enchiladas, rice, chips, dip, and big scoops of ice cream on top of a rich chocolate brownie. But conversation was more important than eating.

Full and happy, the family cleaned up the dining room and tossed paper plates, cups, and plastic eating utensils into the garbage. Martha smiled as she watched her family working together. She couldn't remember having been this happy in a long time.

They naturally migrated to the piano where Susan sat softly playing Christmas carols. The clear, sweet soprano voices of Nancy, Stacey, and Lyric soared above the rest as they sang all their favorite Christmas songs.

When Martha suggested they move into the other room, they did so and settled in around the fireplace while Michael, Bobby, and Steven went outside to bring in more wood.

With the lights of the Christmas tree, flames from the fire, and one small lamp casting shadows on the wall, the group became silent as they gazed at one another. Then Martha asked Bill to read the Christmas story from Luke. Martha knew that her husband John looked down at them and was happy.

The Pettit family returned to the ranch to take care of the stock, promising to return for dinner at two the next day, and beds were found for the family from North Carolina. It was midnight before everyone settled down. Martha quietly tiptoed to each bedroom, knocked lightly, and then whispered "Good night. Merry Christmas."

The lights were off, and Nellie lay in one twin bed and Stacey in the other. Both were silent, lost in their own thoughts as they gazed out the window at the stars, the moon, and the big sky.

"Mom," whispered Stacey, "I'm sorry."

"No, Stacey, I'm the one who is sorry. This was all my fault. Please believe me when I tell you that I have never been ashamed of you. I was ashamed of me. I handled this all wrong from the beginning." A peaceful silence blanketed the room for a few minutes, and then Nellie continued, "Thank you for showing me the way our lives should be. Do you want me to tell you what happened?"

Stacey lay silent for a few minutes, and then stifling a yawn, she whispered, "Maybe some day. Right now I'm just too happy. It's enough that we're here together with our family. Merry Christmas, Mom. I love you."

It was Christmas morning, and everyone slept in. It seemed that any excitement about gifts was overshadowed by the joy of being together. When the kids finally straggled out of their bedrooms, Martha, Susan, and Nellie were busy in the kitchen talking, laughing, and preparing food for Christmas dinner. The smell of hot cinnamon rolls was the magnet that drew the children to the kitchen instead of the tree. After a light breakfast and the gift opening festivities, Stacey, Lyric, and Michael settled down in front of the fireplace to play Kings Around the Corner, wait for the other cousins, and to get further acquainted.

A light snow began to fall, putting a fresh layer on top of the dirty packed snow. Nellie gazed out the window with a smile on her face as she realized that the fresh snow was like her present life. It covered up and hid the old snow just as the present covered up and did away with her old life and old errors. Finally, she realized what Charlotte had meant when she talked about the Atonement.

By the time dinner was over and the dishes were cleaned up, the cousins from North Carolina and California could wait no longer to get out in the snow. Nancy and her brothers had brought all the winter clothing and ice skates they could find with them, and Grandma found a box containing skates and coats used long ago. She had come close to giving them away several times, but was now glad she had kept them.

Bill offered to take the kids to the old ice skating pond a few miles away, but Martha insisted that she wanted to take them. As they were leaving, she pointed to three inconspicuous packages back behind the tree. "Whoops! It looks like we forgot some presents this morning. I think they might be for you, children."

Bill and his sisters smiled at the use of their mother's term—*children*. Bill rose lazily from the love seat where he and Susan had settled and pulled out the presents. It was true. There was one for him, one for Nellie, and one for Charlotte. Bill and Susan curled up in the love seat, Robert and Charlotte occupied the sofa, and Nellie pulled the bean bag chair closer to the fireplace. As one, they all began opening their presents from their mother.

As the "children" opened their packages, they each discovered a letter from their mother, a letter in a sealed envelope from their dad, and a scrapbook made just for them. They looked at each other with a somewhat perplexed expression on their faces; unspoken communication took place, and of one accord they began reading their mother's letter.

Only the crackling of the fire could be heard as they finished reading. Tears glistened in their eyes.

"What in the world?"

"Why would Mom think she owes us an apology?"

"I can't believe she thinks of herself as a failure!"

"I can't believe she's felt this way for so long!"

When Bill asked, "What have we done to make her feel this way?" each one fell silent, searching through memories and realizing that in his or her own way, a relationship with their mother had not been a priority.

"Well," mumbled Charlotte, "let's see what Dad has to say."

Opening up the envelopes that had been sealed for eighteen months, they began to read.

Each envelope contained two letters—one with a special message just for that child, and the other to all of them. Nellie struggled as she read:

> *Dear Nellie,*
>
> *I hope this letter finds you well. Your mother and I regret the way things worked out between us. I am truly sorry I can't hand this to you in person, but I want you to know that I will embrace you with a hug that will make up for all of those that we've missed. I love you so very much!*
>
> *Dad*

Looking up, Nellie realized that her siblings were as touched as she was by the final words of their father to them. Swallowing hard, she turned the page.

> *Dear Children,*
>
> *I am getting old, and I need to leave some thoughts with you. I have always taught you that "Priorities define the man (or woman)." I pray that you will prioritize with the right final goal in mind. You children have always been at the top of our list of priorities, but I'm not sure you have always seen it that way. It is interesting how our perceptions of one another and of situations sometimes get skewed. We have a tendency to look at others and think they are smarter, prettier, loved more, or have a better life, when actually they may be thinking the same about us.*
>
> *As you were growing up, your mother made some tremendous sacrifices for the good of the family, but I'm not sure that you perceived what she was doing as a sacrifice. When we married and moved to the ranch, we had high hopes and big dreams. We were going to make it big. Cattle prices were high at that time, and we were sure we could pay the mortgage off soon. When we were blessed with three*

beautiful children over the next seven years, we thought we had it made. However, by the time you were all in school, cattle prices had dropped, we had a drought, and the price of hay had skyrocketed. We were in deep trouble.

Your mother had enjoyed being a stay-at-home mom. That had always been our plan. However, when the troubles came and we couldn't pay our bills, she gently reminded me that she was a trained nurse. She offered to get a job at the hospital. Then a few years later when we faced more bills (remember when I had that tractor accident and was laid up for a while?) and college and other expenses loomed insurmountably, she picked up a shift or two at "The Hole in the Wall." She pulled us through. It was because of her that I was able to attend all your sporting events and other school activities. I was my own boss. I usually could arrange my work schedule. She didn't have that luxury.

I tell you these things because I feel that you thought her lack of attendance was because of lack of interest or that her jobs were more important than you were. That was not true. Your mother is the most unselfish person in the world. I saw hurt looks on her face and heard her frustration when she wasn't able to be there for you. She cared deeply.

I ask you to see your mother through my eyes. Love her and cherish her. Love and cherish each other. Accept one another with all your imperfections. Take a new look, gain a new perception, and prioritize to include God and family first and foremost.

And please accept my apology for my failures in my life. I will be waiting for you when it's your time.
Love,
Dad

Sniffling and the crackling of the fireplace were the only sounds as each sibling finished reading the letter. They stared into the fire, quietly turned the pages of their scrapbooks, and realized that being sorry but never seeking forgiveness had cost them greatly.

It had cost them time with their siblings, joy with their nieces and nephews, and peace and love with their mother. Through the forgiveness they now found, all was recovered and not lost.

Martha listened to the laughter of her grandchildren. They were teasing and fooling around as if they had spent every day together.

"How much farther, Grandma?"

The inevitable question was asked by Lyric, and Stacey giggled as Michael punched his sister lightly on the shoulder, "Can't we ever go anyplace without you asking that question?"

Bobby and Steven joined in the teasing of their cousin.

Just then the old pond came into view, and Martha pulled to a stop. The children tumbled out of the car, pulled on their skates, gloves, and mufflers in a race to see who would be first on the ice.

Martha had also brought her skates. Many years had passed since she had skated here with her children, and now she was not going to miss this experience with her grandchildren even if she fell down. The grandchildren hooted with delight as they saw that their grandmother was going to join them. Michael and Bobby each chivalrously took one of her hands and led her onto the ice. Martha faltered, and her thoughts went back to the house. "Would her children accept the letters and scrapbooks the way they were intended? Would they understand?" For a moment she wondered what the letters from their father had contained, but then she gave herself up to the joy of the moment.

Bill and Charlotte had been sitting close to their spouses so that they too could read the letters while Nellie savored each word by herself. Now, Bill and Charlotte quietly moved to either side of Nellie, and they shared a group hug, the way they often had when they were children.

Within moments they were communicating the way siblings should. Nellie's memory of the Senior Cotillion came to life as she found the picture of her and Bill ready for the dance. Bill groaned teasingly and said, "Oh, no. I really did take you to that dance. There's the proof!"

It seemed as if they simply couldn't look at the pictures fast enough, and the competition as to who could remember the funniest things about one of the others grew exponentially.

"Hey, enough already," Robert said, laughing as he tugged Charlotte up from the middle of the floor where she was sitting by her siblings. "Why don't we join the others at the ice skating pond before it's too dark?"

"Sounds great! Come on, you guys. You really need to let your mother know how much you appreciate her." Susan smiled at the three siblings. This was the kind of life she envisioned. This was what she wanted for her own children. Glancing at Bill, she knew that the man she had married was really back.

Bill smiled meaningfully at Susan, and then wrapping an arm around each sister, he realized that the three of them were a team again. He felt responsibility as well as relief as he realized that he now had the pleasure of being head of the Day family. "Dad taught us many lessons when he was alive, and he continues to teach me from beyond this life. I hope you will be able to see in me the lessons I have learned from him."

As the five adults began bundling up to face the cold, much warmth emanated from their hearts. Nellie knew what her brother meant. She had been estranged from this feeling for many years. This describable but abstract feeling flared forth from the memories they shared, but it would also ignite future experiences that they would all enjoy together.

Charlotte had never left home but had felt homesickness because of the lost contact with her brother and sister. She now felt as if she were truly home.

*J*anet H. Weaver, the oldest of six children, graduated from Beaver High School, Colorado State University, and Brigham Young Uiversity. She taught speech, drama, journalism, and English at Pleasant Grove High School and Cedar High School.

She and her husband, Kimball, live in Cedar City, Utah, and have seven children: Kim, Cleve, Chris, Wendy, Michael, Amyanne, and Heather. She is now the grandmother of thirty-three and loves being involved in their activities.

A dream at age twelve to publish a book recently became number one on her bucket list, as she and Michael combined to coauthor *The Apology*.

*M*ichael H. Weaver has reawakened to the joys of life as he has taken up his pen to create the many stories he has running around in his brain. He presently has several works in progress.

Michael is married to Ember Graff, and they are the parents of three children: Savana, Solomon, and Kate.

Following his graduation from Cedar High School, he went on a mission to Santa Rosa, California, and then continued his education at Southern Utah University, where he graduated in business. Since then he has had several experiences that have led him to take up writing.

He and his family make their home in Bountiful, Utah, where he is in sales to make a living and writes to make a life.